I0822574

Dedicated to all those who love their life and celebrate it every day more or less on their own.

Copyright©2017 Jerbil,Inc. of New York
All rights reserved. No part of this book may be reproduced or utilized in any form or by any means, electronic or mechanical, photocopying, recording, or by any information storage or retrieval system, without permission in writing from the Publisher.
ISBN 978-0-9715-0571-1
Printed in the United States Of America
First Edition
1 2 3 4 5 6 7 8 9 10
www.jerbilbooks.com

A Man Is An Island

Jeffrey Reid Baker

Illustrated by Les Moore

Jerbil Books
Huntington, New York

There was once a man…

...who was stranded on a
deserted island.

It was a paradise in every sense of the word...

...and so far away from
the things of man.

Wildlife of all kinds became
his constant companions.

The trees gave him shade.

The sun smiled down at
him most days.

The clouds provided water on other days.

The warm wind caressed
his face ever so softly.

There was an abundance of fruits and vegetables.

The birds dazzled him with
their brilliant colors.

The sea waves splashed
with motion and life.

The sky provided a never
ending change of hues.

The night sounds were his lullaby as he slept.

This was a place one could live and be happy forever...

...an Eden if you will.

There was only one thing absent on his island.

There was no religion at all.

www.ingramcontent.com/pod-product-compliance
Lightning Source LLC
Chambersburg PA
CBHW060620310726
48982CB00003B/619
9780971505711